Library of Congress Control Number: 2018914518

ISBN: Softcover   978-1-9845-5094-1
         Hardcover   978-1-9845-5096-5
         EBook   978-1-9845-5095-8

Print information available on the last page.

To order additional copies of this book, contact:
Xlibris
1-888-795-4274
www.Xlibris.com
Orders@Xlibris.com

This book is dedicated to my husband Ramiro,

niece Josephine "Kitty", and all my nephews

and nieces whom I love dearly, plus in loving

memory of my beloved "Chickie"

and my bird "Coo Coo".

VOCABULARY WORDS:

Hopscotch – Played with several players or alone, a playground game in which a player will toss a small object like a simple stone into numbered spaces of a pattern of rectangles outlined on the ground and hop or jump through the spaces to retrieve the object. The pattern can be on dirt on the ground or use a chalk onto a sidewalk.

Hide-and-seek (or go seek) – A game where two or more can play, one player is chosen to be "It" counting to a set number allowing the other players to hide with-in the area and the player "It" attempts to locate all the players. The game can end several ways, one by locating all players and the one found last is the winner, or by having those caught help the players locate the others.

Seesaw – Also known as a teeter-totter, a long flat board that is pivoted in the middle so that one side goes up and the other goes down.

Today was Kitty's first day at school and she could not wait to make new friends.

She tried making friends with Rilely and Brandi but they were too busy playing hopscotch. She went over to Justice and Cain but they were busy helping Mikie catch silly frogs. She looked around and saw Mia, Hunter, and Analia but they were playing hiding go seek with Emmitt, Andrew and Anthony. Kitty wanted to give up, when she saw Adrian and Roxie she headed towards them but they quickly ran to the seesaw. Kitty looked as everyone played around her, and wished she too had a friend. She tried, but everyone was just too busy.

How do you think Kitty is feeling and why?

Kitty walked home from school feeling very sad but as she neared her house she spotted something very colorful and beautiful. She dashed toward it and just as she got close, it flew away. Kitty thought, "If I can only just catch it!" She tried and tried again but each time she was near, it would fly away.

What do you think Kitty is trying to catch?

Kitty headed home in time for dinner. Her mother asked, "Kitty, how was your day?" Kitty replied, "School was fine." But Kitty's mother knew by her voice that all was not well.

What do you think is wrong?

Kitty went to bed thinking about her day and the next morning she woke up ready for a new day. She ate her breakfast, hurried to school and as she walked out the front door she again spotted what she had tried so hard to catch.

She told herself, "When I catch it I will make it my friend."

What do you think she is seeing and trying so hard to catch?

Kitty's mother was watching from the kitchen window when she saw Kitty fall into a flower bed. When she ran outside Kitty was crying, tears running down her face. Kitty looked at mother and cried out, "I just wanted to make it my friend!" Kitty's mother helped her up, wiped away her tears, gave her a hug and sent her on her way to school.

What is Kitty feeling?

When she arrived at school everyone was playing before the school bell rang and again no one seemed to notice her. When the school day ended Kitty was still thinking how she wished she had a friend of her own. She walked outside and saw that her mother was waiting for her. Kitty's mother gave her a smile and said, "I have a surprise for you!" Kitty tried to be happy but she was still thinking how she wished she had a friend.

They drove down the road and came to a stop. Kitty saw they were at the Zoo.

Kitty's mother took her hand, led her to the entrance gate and paid the lady for the tickets. Once inside the zoo, the zoo caretaker was waiting for them and he quickly came to greet them by name. He said, "Good afternoon, Mrs. Cordova and Kitty. I have been expecting you." Then he led them down a long curvy path, as he came to a stop he said, "Kitty you are as beautiful as a butterfly and all its many colors." He winked at her and opened the door.

What do you think Kitty is going to see?

When Kitty entered, she walked into a secret garden of butterflies galore! Kitty could not believe her eyes! She dashed towards them as they all danced around her Kitty chanted, "Oh butterfly, oh butterfly, how beautiful you are. Oh butterfly, oh butterfly the many colors that you wear. Oh butterfly, oh butterfly won't you be a friend of mine?"

Kitty's mother once again took her hand, and whispered ever so gently, "Be still my little one and see what awaits you." Kitty stood still, as the butterflies danced all around her; they landed on her shoulder, her hair, arm, and even on her nose! Kitty was so tickled yet she stood still as could be. She then looked toward her mother and smiled as she dashed toward her to give her a BIG hug!

Kitty chanted, *"Oh butterfly, oh butterfly, how beautiful you are. Oh butterfly, oh butterfly the many colors that you wear. Oh butterfly, oh butterfly are you a friend of mine?"*

How do you think Kitty is feeling now?

Kitty went to school the next day and she stood still, as one by one all the children in her class came by to play with her. Oh, the many friends that Kitty made!

BUT little did Kitty know that on her way home from school awaited an even BIGGER surprise!

What do you think is the bigger surprise?

Kitty was walking home when she saw someone catching what she tried so hard to catch. She shook her head and smiled as she went towards her new friend. Jordan was chasing butterflies. Kitty took Jordan by the hand and whispered in his ear, "Be still my friend" *and a beautiful colorful butterfly landed gently on their hand.* Kitty chanted softly, "Oh *butterfly, oh butterfly the many colors that you wear. Oh butterfly, oh butterfly YOU ARE a friend of mine.*"

So what was Kitty seeing that she tried to catch and how do you think she feels now?